DISNEY

CLASSIC
POOH

Pooh's School Day

by Lauren Cecil
illustrated by Andrew Grey

Grosset & Dunlap
An Imprint of Penguin Group (USA) Inc.

ISBN 978-0-448-45414-6   10 9 8 7 6 5 4 3 2 1

On a wet, cloudy day in the Hundred Acre Wood,
Owl visited Winnie-the-Pooh at his house.

"It's too rainy to go outside and play," said Pooh.

"Indeed it is," Owl agreed.

Owl thought for a moment, then said, "I've got an
idea! Get little Piglet and meet me at my house."

Pooh arrived at Owl's house with Piglet in tow.

He saw Rabbit, Eeyore, Tigger, and Roo sitting on the floor.

He rubbed his nose and thought very hard.

I wonder what we are doing?

"Hallo, Pooh! Hallo, Piglet! Today we are going to play school," Owl said. "And I shall be the teacher." "Wonderful!" Pooh replied.

"But aren't there tests in school?" Piglet asked.

"Perhaps," Owl replied. "But if you pay attention, you will do fine."

Tests sounded scary, but Piglet decided to be brave.

"I'll be ready for them," Piglet said. "Just make sure they're not *too* hard."

"Let's begin with some math," Owl said. "What is two plus two?"

Pooh raised his hand. "Eleven," he said.

"Almost, but not quite," Owl replied. "The answer is four."

"What I meant to say was that it is eleven o'clock. And I always like a little snack at eleven," said Pooh. Then he took out a honey-pot and began eating loudly.

"Let's move on to the alphabet," Owl said. "What comes after *A, B,* and *C*?"

"WHEE!" Tigger shouted as he bounced around the room.

"Almost, but not quite," said Owl. "The correct answer is *D*. Shall we continue?"

"But bouncing is so much fun!" Tigger cried.

"How about some spelling," Owl said. "*C-U-P* spells . . ."

"*Hic-cup!*" Roo squeaked.

"Almost, but not quite," said Owl, somewhat surprised.

"*Hiccup!*" Roo squeaked again.

"Oh dear," Owl said. "I believe you have a case of the hiccups!"

With Piglet fretting about a test, Pooh eating, Tigger bouncing, and Roo hiccupping, no one was listening to Owl at all.

"Everyone be QUIET!" Rabbit hollered. "I say, quiet!"
"Thank you, Rabbit," said Owl. "Now, as I was
saying . . ."

Eeyore interrupted by raising a hoof.

"Yes, Eeyore?" Owl asked.

"This is not a very good game at all," Eeyore said glumly.

"But why not?" Owl asked. "I find playing school to be quite enjoyable."

Just then a visitor appeared. It was Christopher Robin.

"Hallo, everyone!" he said. "What are you doing?"

"We're playing school," Owl said. "Or trying to . . ."

"Do you know what my favorite part of school is?" Christopher Robin asked.

Everyone shook their heads.

"Recess!" he said. "That's when you go outside and play!"
Everyone agreed that recess sounded like a grand idea.
"But isn't it too rainy to play outside?" Pooh asked.
"The rain has stopped," Christopher Robin said. "See?"

"Well, in that case," Owl began, "class dismissed!"
They all went outside to play and had a marvelous time.

While everyone played outside, Piglet asked
Pooh, "What did you think of school today?"
"I rather liked it," said Pooh. "But I thought
recess should have started much sooner."